For Jason, my forever friend
~ CF
For Anna, with all my love
~ BC

SIMON AND SCHUSTER

First published in Great Britain in 2007 by Simon & Schuster UK Ltd
Africa House, 64-78 Kingsway, London WC2B 6AH
A CBS COMPANY

Book designed by Genevieve Webster
The text for this book is set in Jerky Tash
The illustrations are rendered in acrylics

A CIP catalogue record for this book is available from
the British Library upon request

ISBN 978-1-4169-1705-2

Printed in China

15 17 19 20 18 16 14

Aliens Love Underpants

Claire Freedman & Ben Cort

SIMON AND SCHUSTER

London   New York   Sydney

Aliens love underpants,
Of every shape and size.
But there are no underpants in space,
So here's a big surprise...

When aliens fly down to Earth,
They don't come to meet YOU...
They simply want your underpants –
I'll bet you never knew!

Their spaceship's radar bleeps and blinks
The moment that it sees
A washing line of underpants,
All flapping in the breeze.

They land in your back garden,
Though they haven't been invited.
"Oooooh, UNDERPANTS!" they chant,
And dance around, delighted.

They like them red, they like them green,
Or orange like satsumas.
But best of all they love the sight,
Of Granny's spotted bloomers.

Mum's pink frilly knickers
Are a perfect place to hide
And Grandpa's woolly longjohns
Make a super-whizzy slide.

In daring competitions,
Held up by just one peg,
They count how many aliens
Can squeeze inside each leg.

They wear pants on their feet and heads
And other silly places.
They fly pants from their spaceships and
Hold Upside-Down-Pant Races!

As they go zinging through the air,
It really is pants-tastic.
What fun the aliens can have,
With pingy pants elastic!

It's not your neighbour's naughty dog,
Or next-door's funny game.
When underpants go missing,
The ALIENS are to blame!

But quick! Mum's coming out to fetch
The washing in at last.
Wheee! Off the aliens all zoom,
They're used to leaving fast...

So when you put your pants on,
Freshly washed and nice and clean,
Just check in case an alien
Still lurks inside, unseen!